Run, Little CHASKi!

AN INKA TRAiL ADVENTURE

written by **Mariana Llanos**

illustrated by **Mariana Ruiz Johnson**

Barefoot Books
Step inside a story

Little Chaski wakes up before Tayta Inti shines in the sky. Little Chaski's stomach twists. It is his first day delivering royal messages. Will he be a good messenger?

"Be sure to be strong," says Brave Chaski, his older brother.

"Be sure to be swift," says Big Chaski, his father.

"Be sure to be sharp," says Wise Chaski, his grandfather.

Little Chaski receives his mission from the Qoya, the Queen, herself:

"This khipu is very important. Bring it to the Inka, the King, at the temple before Tayta Inti sets behind those mountains. Do not be late!"

"Yes, great Qoya. I won't disappoint," says Little Chaski, ready to move his legs fast as a puma.

With a ch'uspa full of jerky and kamcha for a snack, and a gleaming white pututu hanging on his side, Little Chaski starts his long journey.

Chakiti, chakiti. His sandals strike the ground as he runs on the Qhapaq Ñan, the Inka Trail, leaving the Qoya's palace behind.

Run, run, Little Chaski, phaway!

But as Little Chaski races, a chinchilla crosses the road and —

Smack!

Kapum!

What a mess!

Little Chaski's knees are sore, but he decides to be strong. Chinchilla looks even worse.

"Are you okay, friend?"

Little Chaski helps Chinchilla and soon he is back on the road.

Oh no! . . . Tayta Inti has tiptoed to the west.

"I must move as fast as a waterfall!" exclaims Little Chaski.

Run, run, Little Chaski, phaway!

But as Little Chaski darts downhill, a wail pierces his ears. It comes from the river —

Squee!

Shrrr!

An allqu is in trouble!
Little Chaski decides to help.

Little Chaski tosses his ch'uspa. Allqu grabs.
With a swift movement, Allqu is back on land!

Allqu shakes. Little Chaski pats her head and then
jumps back on the road.

Oh no! Tayta Inti has slid closer to the west.

"I must run faster than the wind!" exclaims Little Chaski.

Run, run, Little
Chaski, phaway!

But something brushes the bushes and —
it's a condor! He fluffs his feathers. He grunts.

Condor is trapped and scared!

Little Chaski must be sharp. He tosses a rock to distract the bird.

While Condor looks away, Little Chaski rushes to the branch and . . . *zas!* Condor is free!

"Fly away, friend," says Little Chaski as he darts back on the road.

Oh no! Tayta Inti is about to dive behind the mountain!

"I must fly faster than a shooting star!" exclaims Little Chaski.

Run, run, Little Chaski, phaway!

Zoom, zoom up the mountain.

Clac, clac past the pond.

Chis, chis past a herd of vicuñas eating grass.

Little Chaski is almost there. *Chakiti, chakiti,* his sandals slam on the steps. He shoots through the temple doorway just as Tayta Inti's last rays sink behind the mountains.

Little Chaski takes a minute to catch his breath. Then, he grabs his pututu and blows. Now everyone knows he is there!

"What message have you brought?" asks the Inka.

Little Chaski reaches in his ch'uspa — *chiss, chass.* How could this be? His bag is empty!

The Inka taps his foot. The Reader of the Khipu scowls. *Boom.* Little Chaski's heart pounds!

"Where is the khipu?" demands the frowning Inka.

But just when Little Chaski's cheeks turn red as a huayruro seed, three grateful friends soar from the clouds and —

Swish!

Zoom!

The message falls into Little Chaski's hands!

Little Chaski is relieved, but the Inka wants to know more. So, Little Chaski tells him the story of how he helped the animals along the way. The Inka listens and smiles while the Reader of the Khipu examines the message.

Then the Inka says, "Little Chaski, this was a test for you. You're now an official Chaski of the Tawantinsuyu. On your journey you remembered to be strong, swift and sharp. But you were something even more important: you were kind. And because of your actions, I shall give you your name: Big-Hearted Chaski."

Everyone cheers. And Big-Hearted Chaski's smile glows brighter than Tayta Inti.

Glossary of Quechua words:

✷ allqu *(AL-koo)*:
a hairless dog found in Peru

✷ chaski *(CHAS-key)*:
a royal messenger during Inka times

✷ chinchilla *(chin-CHEE-yah)*:
a rabbit-like animal found in the
Andes Mountains

✷ ch'uspa *(CHOOS-pah)*:
a bag used in the Andes region to
carry coca leaves and other items

✷ condor *(KON-dor)*:
a vulture found in the Andes
Mountains that is the largest flying
bird in the western hemisphere

✷ huayruro *(why-ROO-roh)*:
a plant native to Peru, with seeds
that are bright red with a black spot

✷ Inka *(EEN-kah)*:
the king of the Inka Empire

✷ kamcha *(KAM-chah)*:
a toasted corn snack

✷ khipu *(KEE-poo)*:
a recording system made of rope
and hanging knotted threads

✷ phaway! *(PAH-why)*:
run!

✷ puma *(POO-mah)*:
a cat-like animal found in the
Andes Mountains

✷ pututu *(poo-TOO-too)*:
a musical instrument made of a
giant seashell used by chaskis to
announce their arrival

✷ Qhapaq Ñan *(KAH-pak nyahn)*:
the Inka Trail, a system of roads

✷ Qoya *(KOH-yah)*:
queen, wife of the Inka

✷ Tayta Inti *(TAI-tah IN-tee)*:
father Sun

✷ vicuña *(vee-KOON-yah)*:
an animal related to llamas and
alpacas that lives in the Andes

Who were the Inka?

The Inka were a society that ruled the Andes Mountains of South America until after the invasion of the Spanish conquistadors in 1532 CE. Their empire was called Tawantinsuyu, which means Four Regions. Their capital was the city of Cusco. The Inka were skilled builders, engineers and warriors. Their palaces, temples and other developments still impress visitors today.

Drawing of a chaski by Felipe Guaman Poma de Ayala, drawn between 1600 and 1615 CE

Who were the chaskis?

The chaskis were fleet-footed couriers who delivered important messages, news or packages in a relay system throughout the vast territory of the Tawantinsuyu. Boys trained from a young age to be chaskis. They had to be strong, since they ran long distances on difficult roads. Chaskis ran on the Inka Trail, known as Qhapaq Ñan, an advanced system of roads that connected the Tawantinsuyu. If you visit countries in South America, you can still find parts of these roads.

What did the chaskis deliver?

One of the things chaskis delivered was khipus (or quipus). A khipu was a recording device made of a cord and knotted threads of different types. Khipus were used to keep tally and record other important events. Only a few people were able to read the khipus. They were called khipukamayuq and they were specially educated for the job.

COLOMBIA

VENEZUELA

GUYANA

SURINAME

FRENCH GUIANA

ECUADOR

BRAZIL

PERU

THE
INKA
EMPIRE
at its largest size
around 1525 CE

BOLIVIA

PARAGUAY

CHILE

ARGENTINA

URUGUAY

The Inka Empire

The Inka Empire was once
the largest civilization in the
Americas. The ruler of the
Tawantinsuyu was also called
"the Inka" and was believed to be
the child of the Sun. Quechua was
the official language, but many
other languages were spoken
across their empire too. The Inka
did not have a written language.
Machu Picchu, a beautiful ancient
city between the Andes Mountains
and the Amazon Basin in Peru,
is one of the most famous
surviving Inka sites.

Inka or Inca?

When Spanish conquistadors
invaded the Inka Empire,
they used their own language
to describe the local people.
Spanish spellings of Quechua
words became the norm. Today,
the languages and thoughts
of Indigenous people are
recognized. In this book, we
use the Quechua spelling Inka,
though the Spanish spelling,
Inca, is still common.

The Inka Trail

The Inka Trail, or Qhapaq Ñan, was used for official government and military business, and perhaps for religious pilgrimages as well. Two long roads ran north to south along the coast and within the mountains, and various roads connected them. Parts of the Trail included tunnels through mountains and various bridges. The roads also had rest stations along the way.

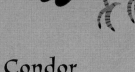

Animals in South America

  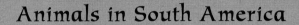

Chinchilla

A chinchilla is a rodent from the Andes Mountains with very soft fur and rounded ears.

Allqu

The allqu, a Peruvian hairless dog sometimes believed to have healing powers, has been a popular pet since before the Inka Empire.

Condor

The condor is a vulture, one of the world's biggest flying animals, with a wingspan the size of a small car!

Growing up in Peru, I was always proud of our history — both the Inka Empire and the rich pre-Inka cultures. The Inka accomplished a lot in a fairly short amount of time. Instead of destroying other cultures when they took over lands, they learned from the people they conquered. They built their amazing constructions without wheels or iron tools. I love the way they respected nature and built things that are in harmony with the landscape. I hope readers will be inspired to learn more about the largest empire in the Americas.

— Mariana Llanos

When I was eighteen years old, I explored Bolivia and Peru by bus with two friends. We hiked and camped along the real Inka Trail to reach Machupicchu. I was fascinated by the landscape and culture. I enjoyed diving into Inka culture to create the illustrations for this book. For inspiration, I looked at photographs from my many travels, and Peruvian folk arts like pottery, textiles, wood altars and goldsmithing.

— Mariana Ruiz Johnson

To Wiracocha, without whom the Inka world would not have been created, and to my mom and dad, without whom this book wouldn't either — M. L.

To my kids, Pepo and Felix — M. R. J.

Barefoot Books
23 Bradford Street, 2nd Floor
Concord, MA 01742

Barefoot Books
29/30 Fitzroy Square
London, W1T 6LQ

Edited and art directed by Kate DePalma, Barefoot Books
Reproduction by Bright Arts, Hong Kong. Printed in China
This book was typeset in Amigo, Caudex and Plantin Schoolbook
The illustrations were prepared in
mixed media combined with digital techniques

ISBN 978-1-64686-858-2

British Cataloguing-in-Publication Data: a catalogue
record for this book is available from the British Library

Library of Congress Cataloging-in-Publication Data
is available under LCCN 2020951322

1 3 5 7 9 8 6 4 2

Graphic design by Elizabeth Jayasekera, Barefoot Books